The Pony and the Haunted Barn

Do you love ponies? Be a Pony Pal!

PONY PALS

The Pony and the Haunted Barn

Jeanne Betancourt

Illustrated by Richard Jones

A
LITTLE APPLE
PAPERBACK

SCHOLASTIC INC.
New York   Toronto   London   Auckland   Sydney
Mexico City   New Delhi   Hong Kong   Buenos Aires

ISBN 0-439-42625-1

Copyright © 2002 by Jeanne Betancourt.
All rights reserved. Published by Scholastic Inc.

SCHOLASTIC, LITTLE APPLE, and associated logos are trademarks and/or registered trademarks of Scholastic Inc.

12 11 10 9 8 7 6 5 4 3 2 1   2 3 4 5 6 7/0

Printed in the U.S.A.   40
First Scholastic printing, September 2002

Contents

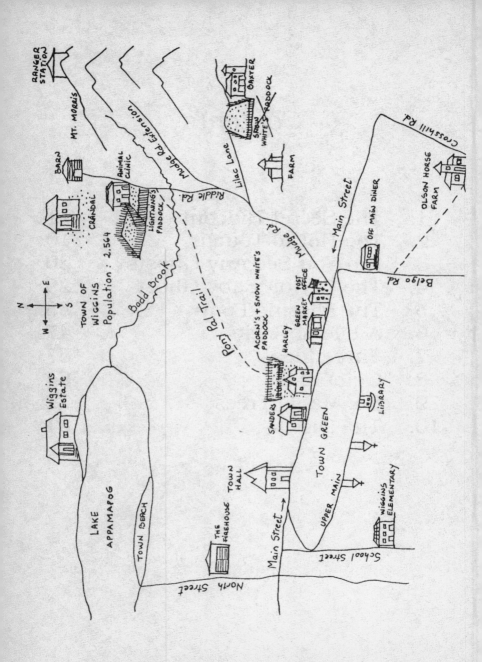

The Secret Hideout

Pam Crandal threw her raincoat on over her pajamas. She looked at the kitchen clock. It was five minutes before midnight. Thunder rumbled in the distance.

Pam ran out of the house and into the storm. Rain splashed off her coat and slashed at her face. As she rushed toward the paddock, she felt something brush by her. She looked around, but nothing was there.

A shiver of fear ran through Pam. There's nothing to be afraid of, she scolded herself. I must have imagined it. But she still couldn't shake the scary feeling in the pit of her stomach.

Pam took a deep breath and opened the paddock gate. "Come on, Lightning," she yelled. "I'm going to put you in the barn."

Lightning galloped across the paddock to her.

Pam led her wet pony into the barn and rubbed her down. Lightning nickered a thank-you and nuzzled her shoulder.

"I hope the rain stops soon," Pam told her pony. "We're supposed to go on a long trail ride with our Pony Pals tomorrow." She stroked Lightning's white upside-down heart marking for good luck.

The next morning, bright sunshine filled Pam's bedroom. She looked out at a clear, blue-sky day. I was silly to be afraid last night, she told herself.

By ten o'clock the next morning, Anna Harley, Lulu Sanders, and their ponies were at the Crandals'. Everyone was ready for a Pony Pal trail ride and picnic.

Pam had apples and juice boxes in her saddlebag. "Did you bring brownies?" she asked Anna.

"Lots," answered Anna. "And some jelly beans."

Anna's Shetland pony, Acorn, whinnied as if to say, "Goody. Jelly beans."

Anna leaned forward in the saddle and patted Acorn's neck. "They're not for you, silly," she said. "Pam has an apple for you."

"I've got the sandwiches," Lulu said as she mounted her Welsh pony, Snow White. "Peanut butter and jelly."

Acorn nuzzled Lulu's shoulder. "Those aren't for you, either, Acorn," Lulu told the mischievous pony.

The Pony Pals had red whistles hanging around their necks. The whistles were for safety. If the girls got separated they could signal one another.

Pam mounted Lightning. "I want to go for a really long ride today," she said.

"Where should we go?" asked Anna.

"Let's go to Morristown," suggested Lulu.

Morristown was a ghost town. Nobody had lived there for more than a hundred years, and none of the buildings were still standing. All that was left were piles of rocks where houses and barns used to be. Sometimes the Pony Pals found relics from the past there.

Their favorite site in Morristown was the Ridley Farm Ruin. "Riding to Morristown is a great idea, Lulu," said Anna. "Is that okay with you, Pam?"

"Sure," agreed Pam. She didn't tell Anna and Lulu about her spooky experience in the storm.

Pam led the way down Riddle Road. They made a left onto Mudge Road Extension. Soon they came to the Morristown Trail.

It was a beautiful day for a ride in the woods. There were orange and red autumn leaves on the trees. I love fall the best for riding, thought Pam.

When the Pony Pals reached Morristown, Lightning suddenly stopped. She turned to her left and sniffed curiously.

"What did Lightning find?" asked Lulu.

"I don't know," answered Pam. She gave her pony a loose rein. "Let's see what she does."

Lightning walked off the trail. Pam looked ahead to see where her pony was going.

"There's another trail in here," Pam called to her friends.

Lulu rode behind Pam. "We've never been this way before," she said.

Anna moved Acorn onto the path, too. "Wow!" she said. "A new trail. Let's explore it."

The three riders rode slowly. "This is great," observed Pam. "I wonder how we missed it before."

Suddenly, Acorn whinnied and turned in a circle. "Whoa," Anna commanded.

"That's weird," said Lulu. "Acorn never spooks."

"Maybe a bee stung him," said Pam.

Anna leaned forward and rubbed Acorn's withers. "It's okay," she told her pony.

When Acorn calmed down, the girls rode

on. After a short distance the trail narrowed. But it was still easy to ride on.

The narrow trail ended at a row of maple trees. There was a small field beyond the trees. An old stone-and-wood barn stood at the far end of the field.

When Lightning noticed the barn, she shied. Pam reined her pony in. "Don't be afraid," she said. "It's just a barn."

Lulu and Anna rode up beside Pam.

Acorn looked at the barn and nickered as if to say, "What's that?"

"It's a *real* building!" exclaimed Anna. "In Morristown."

The Pony Pals rode side by side up to the barn.

Lulu looked around. "There's no house," she observed. "Just a barn. And the field is overgrown."

The girls tied their ponies to the hitching post in front of the barn.

"I didn't see any 'no trespassing' signs," said Pam. "Let's look inside."

Lulu pulled on the barn door. It creaked open.

"Don't close the door," whispered Anna as they walked inside. "This place gives me the creeps."

There were four stalls in the barn — two on each side of a wide aisle.

"Let's check out the tack room," said Pam.

Pam went in first. She noticed a big trunk, three grain barrels, and two sawhorses. She carefully opened the trunk while Lulu checked out the grain barrels. They were all empty.

"There isn't any tack on the walls," said Anna. "No saddles or bridles. Nothing."

"No one has used this barn in a long time," observed Pam.

"It would make a perfect Pony Pal club-house," said Lulu.

"Let's call it the 'Pony Pals' Secret Barn,'" said Pam. "We can have meetings and picnics here."

"Okay," agreed Anna and Lulu in unison.

"We can put our ponies in the stalls," said Lulu. "It's perfect for wintertime."

"Let's eat our picnic in here," added Pam.

"Oh," whimpered Anna. She grabbed Pam's arm. Pam turned to Anna. Anna's eyes were wide with fear.

"What happened?" asked Pam.

"Something touched me," whispered Anna. "Like a person or an animal. It almost pushed me over."

The open barn door suddenly shut with a bang.

Outside, Lightning neighed fearfully.

"Let's go," shouted Lulu as she rushed toward the barn door.

All three ponies were whinnying.

"The door's stuck," shouted Lulu.

Pam and Lulu pulled at the door together. It opened so suddenly they both fell backward.

They jumped up and ran out of the barn.

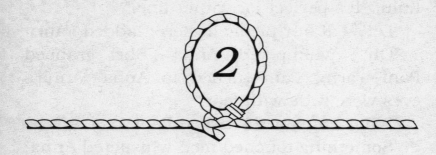

Too Hot To Touch

The Pony Pals hurried over to their frightened ponies.

Snow White had a wild look in her eyes. Acorn pawed the ground. Lightning pulled on the lead rope.

Lulu looked around as she stroked Snow White's neck. "I wonder what upset them," she said.

"That door banging shut," said Pam.

"But why did the door slam?" asked Lulu.

"The wind," answered Pam.

"And what pushed Anna?" asked Lulu.

"That was the wind, too," said Pam matter-of-factly.

Lulu held up her hand to feel the air. "Pam, there is no wind," she said. "The air isn't moving."

"A ghost went by me," whispered Anna. "I know it was a ghost. That barn is haunted."

Acorn nodded his head as if to agree.

"There *are* lots of ghost stories about Morristown," said Lulu. She looked around nervously.

"There are no such things as ghosts," insisted Pam. "We were having so much fun. Don't let ghost stories ruin it."

"That barn *would* make a great clubhouse," said Lulu cautiously.

"Let's go back inside," suggested Pam. "We'll bring the ponies with us this time." She put a hand on Anna's arm. "Okay?"

"Okay," agreed Anna.

Pam led Lightning into the barn. Pam remembered how she was spooked the night before. She pushed the memory away.

Acorn walked in behind Lightning.

Shy Snow White stopped at the door. Acorn turned to her and nickered as if to say, "Come on in."

Snow White cautiously stepped into the barn.

Pam carefully closed the door behind them. She didn't want it to bang shut again and frighten the ponies.

While the girls put their ponies in the stalls and fed them apples, Pam thought about her Pony Pals.

Anna had always believed in ghosts. When she was little she saw a ghost float out her bedroom window. She even drew a picture of it. Pam thought the ghost was in Anna's imagination.

Anna had a great imagination, and she was an excellent artist. But reading and mathematics were difficult for her because she was dyslexic. Anna doesn't like school as much as I do, thought Pam.

The Pony Pals all loved being outdoors with their ponies. And they all loved nature and animals. Pam's father was a veterinarian and her mother gave horseback riding lessons. I know the most about ponies, dogs, and cats, thought Pam. But Lulu knows the most about wild animals and camping out.

Lulu's father traveled all over the world to study wild animals. Her mother died when Lulu was little. After that, Lulu traveled with her father and studied animals, too. When she turned ten, her father said Lulu had to live in one place for a while. That's when Lulu moved to Wiggins and became a Pony Pal. She lived with her grandmother Sanders in the house next to Anna's. When Lulu's father wasn't traveling for work, he lived there, too.

Lulu wasn't sure if she believed in ghosts. "I do and I don't," she once told Pam.

Now Lulu leaned on the half door to Snow White's stall. "Let's have our picnic over here," she suggested.

"We can sit on that old trunk," added Anna.

Anna and Lulu carried the trunk out of the tack room and put it in the barn aisle.

Lulu pointed to some lettering on the front of the wooden trunk. "Something is printed on here," she said.

Pam knelt in front of the trunk. "W-A-R-N-E-R," she read out loud.

"Warner," said Lulu. "A Mr. Warner must have owned the barn."

"Or a woman named Warner," added Pam.

The girls sat on the Warner trunk and ate their sandwiches.

Pam pointed her juice box at a horseshoe hanging over the doorway. "Look," she said. "Warner hung up a horseshoe for good luck."

"I hope he — or she — had good luck," said Lulu.

"This barn doesn't feel lucky to me," said Anna.

Acorn reached his head over the stall door and nuzzled her hair. Anna reached up and patted her pony's neck. Acorn quickly snatched a half of sandwich from her other hand.

"Acorn!" shouted Anna. "That's my sandwich."

Pam and Lulu laughed. "I guess the barn *isn't* lucky for you, Anna," teased Pam.

Acorn nickered happily. "But it's lucky for Acorn," said Anna with a giggle.

Pam and Lulu shared the rest of their sandwiches with Anna.

"I wonder how long this barn has been here," said Lulu as she passed Pam the bag of brownies.

"Maybe there's a clue on the horseshoe," said Pam. "I'll get it down."

The girls pushed the trunk to the doorway and tipped it on its side. Anna and Lulu held the trunk still. Pam stepped on it, stretched out her arm, and reached for the horseshoe.

"Ouch!" she exclaimed as she half jumped and half fell off the trunk.

Lightning whinnied and pawed the floor.

"What happened?" shouted Anna.

"Are you all right?" asked Lulu.

"That horseshoe is hot," explained Pam. She shook her hand.

"Spooky," said Lulu.

"The Warner ghost did it!" exclaimed Anna.

Pam felt annoyed with her friends. "Everything that happens in the world isn't caused by ghosts," she said. "There's a logical explanation for a hot horseshoe."

"What is it?" asked Lulu.

"The sun was shining on it," answered Pam. "Metal gets hot."

"The sun isn't even shining in here, Pam," said Anna. "Look how cloudy it is outside."

Pam saw storm clouds gathering through the barn window.

"Even if the sun *was* shining," explained Lulu, "it wouldn't shine on the horseshoe. The sun shines from the south at this time of day. All the windows are facing north and east."

"I'm *sure* there's a logical explanation," repeated Pam angrily. "You're not even trying to think of one."

Lightning bumped against the side of her stall and whinnied again.

Lulu put her hands on her hips. "Don't get

grumpy with us," she told Pam. "We didn't do anything."

"The ghost did it," added Anna, "not us."

"Stop talking to me about ghosts!" shouted Pam. "I'm taking Lightning outside."

"Let's get ready to go, Lulu," said Anna. "There might be another storm coming."

"Good idea, Anna," agreed Lulu.

Pam went into Lightning's stall. They're ignoring me, she thought. But I don't care. I'm sick of all their talk about ghosts. It's silly. She led Lightning out of the barn through the door in her stall.

As Pam closed the door behind her, she blinked. It was very sunny out. She looked up at the sky. There wasn't a cloud in sight.

I just saw clouds a minute ago, she thought. Where did they go?

Suddenly, Pam heard a clinking sound coming from the woods. Lightning whinnied and backed up. Pam led her in a circle to calm her down.

Clink, clink. The sound was closer.

Lightning suddenly stumbled and whinnied fearfully.

"Whoa!" shouted Pam. She blew one blast on her whistle.

Anna and Lulu rushed out of the barn to see what had happened.

"I heard something," Pam explained. Her voice was shaking. "It was a clinking, clanging sound. Like a chain. Then Lightning stumbled."

"It was the ghost," said Anna in a hoarse whisper. "That ghost doesn't want us in this barn or anywhere near it."

3

Did You See Any Ghosts?

Pam checked to see if Lightning was injured while Anna and Lulu quickly led their ponies out of the barn. "She's okay," Pam announced to her friends.

The three girls stood very still and listened for the clinking noise. They heard *Rat-tat-tat, rat-tat-tat.*

"That's a woodpecker," said Lulu. "Is that the sound you heard, Pam?"

"No," answered Pam. "But maybe I heard another kind of bird."

"Have you ever heard a bird that sounded like a chain?" asked Anna.

"No," admitted Pam. "But I don't listen to birds that much."

"Something weird is going on," said Anna. She tightened Acorn's girth. "Let's get out of here."

"Okay," agreed Lulu as she pulled down her stirrups.

"I'll get our stuff from the barn," offered Pam. "You two stay with the ponies." She headed back to the barn.

Lulu gently ran her hand along Lightning's side. "Lightning's been spooked a lot today," Pam heard Lulu say.

Pam didn't want her friends to know that she was spooked, too. But her heart was pounding as she quickly packed up the empty juice containers and plastic wrap. I do not believe in ghosts, Pam told herself. I do not believe in ghosts.

A few minutes later, the three friends mounted their ponies.

"Lulu, you have the best sense of direction," said Anna. "You lead."

"Okay," agreed Lulu. "We'll go back the way we came." She pointed to a row of sugar maple trees. "We came out over there."

The Pony Pals rode single file between two of the maple trees and onto the trail. They rode for a long time.

Lightning was skittish and kept tugging at the reins.

"Shouldn't we be on the wide trail already?" Pam called to Lulu.

"I think we're almost there," Lulu shouted back.

A few minutes later, Lulu suddenly halted Snow White. She turned in the saddle to face her friends.

Pam noticed that Lulu looked worried. "What's wrong, Lulu?" she asked.

"We're back where we started," answered Lulu.

Pam and Anna rode up beside Lulu.

Between the tree trunks, Pam saw a small field. At the end of the field she saw the

Warner barn. "We must have gone in a circle," she said.

Lulu looked from Anna to Pam. "I'm sorry," she said. "I thought I knew the way."

"You never get lost, Lulu," said Anna.

"I should have drawn a map," said Lulu.

"Let's make one now," suggested Pam as she slid off Lightning.

Lulu and Anna dismounted, too.

"I have my notebook and a pencil," Pam told Lulu.

Lulu took a small compass out of her saddlebag. "The first thing we need to figure out is north, south, east, and west," she explained. She moved the compass to face north. Anna wrote "N" on the map. The girls worked together to make the map as accurate as possible.

Lulu looked at their map. "Okay," she said. "Let's try again."

As the Pony Pals rode back onto the narrow trail, Pam was worried. What if they were really lost?

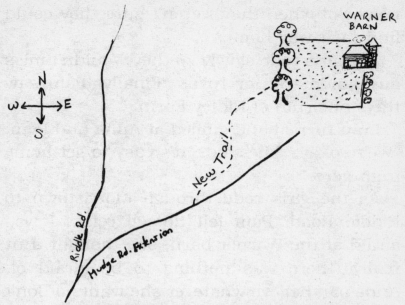

Lulu stopped frequently to check her compass and the map.

Finally, the riders came to a wider trail.

Pam rode up beside Lulu. "This looks right," Lulu announced.

"Then we should be at Ridley Farm soon," said Pam.

"At least the ghosts at Ridley Farm are friendly," added Anna.

Lulu and Pam exchanged a glance. They silently agreed not to talk about ghosts. Not now. Not when they weren't sure they could find their way home.

The girls rode slowly so they wouldn't miss any landmarks or turns. Finally, Pam saw the stone ruin of Ridley Farm.

Lulu turned and smiled at Anna and Pam. "We're okay," she said. "It's easy to get home from here."

As the girls rode through Morristown to Riddle Road, Pam felt herself relax. I was afraid at the Warner barn, she thought. But really, there was nothing to be afraid of. Anna can believe whatever she wants. I don't believe in ghosts.

The Crandal twins — five-year-old Jack and Jill — were playing near the new barn. They helped the Pony Pals cool down their ponies and put them in the paddock. Pam was glad the twins were there. Anna and Lulu wouldn't talk about ghosts in front of them.

"We're having a barbecue," Jill announced

cheerfully. She jumped on Pam's back. "Mom said you have to help."

Pam put dishes, drinks, mustard, relish, catsup, and a bowl of chips on the picnic table. She also helped her mother cook burgers and hot dogs on the grill. Anna and Lulu helped Dr. Crandal make the potato salad and a green salad.

The twins ran around the yard playing catch with the Crandals' dog, Woolie.

It was dark out when they finished eating. Mrs. Crandal took the twins inside for bed. Dr. Crandal's face glowed in the orange light of the grill. Light danced off Lulu's and Anna's faces, too.

Pam looked toward the paddock. The only pony she could see clearly in the dark was Snow White. She looked like a ghost pony. A shiver of fear ran up Pam's spine. She remembered the night before. What bumped into me? she wondered.

"You girls see any ghosts in Morristown?" Dr. Crandal asked.

Pam felt another shiver. Could her father read her mind?

"I felt a ghost brush by me, Dr. Crandal," answered Anna. She rubbed her arm.

Dr. Crandal stirred up the fire. "That doesn't surprise me," he said. "There are a lot of ghosts in Morristown."

Pam stared at her father. Did he believe in ghosts?

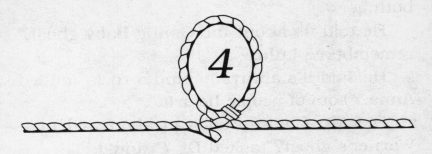

The Crying Baby Ghost

Pam moved closer to her father and the light of the fire.

"Will you tell us a ghost story?" Anna asked Dr. Crandal.

Dr. Crandal's face looked spooky in the firelight. "Do you girls know any of the Morristown ghost stories?" he asked.

"Mr. Conway told us some once," said Lulu. "His family used to live in Morristown."

"William Conway likes to tell ghost stories as much as he likes to shoe ponies," commented Dr. Crandal. "He's an expert on both."

"He told us about the Crying Baby ghost," remembered Lulu.

"He said it's always behind a rock," added Anna. "Lots of people hear it."

"Did Mr. Conway tell you about old man Warner's ghost?" asked Dr. Crandal.

The girls exchanged a glance. They were all thinking the same thing. *Warner* was the name on the tack trunk. They'd been in Warner's barn. They silently agreed not to tell Dr. Crandal.

"What about the Warner ghost?" asked Pam. She wanted to sound relaxed, but her voice was shaking.

"People hear him in the woods around Morristown," he answered. "They say he's dragging a chain. It makes a clanking sound."

Anna grabbed Pam's arm and whispered, "That's what you heard."

"Sh-sh," Pam whispered in Anna's ear. "Don't tell."

"Do you know anything else about the Warner ghost?" asked Lulu.

"He trips up people and horses," answered Dr. Crandal.

The Pony Pals exchanged a glance. They all remembered the same thing at the same time. Mr. Conway *had* told them about the Warner ghost. They'd just forgotten his name.

"Do you believe in the Warner ghost, Dr. Crandal?" asked Lulu. "I mean, that there's a ghost that does those things?"

If my father believes in ghosts, thought Pam, I will, too. "Do you believe in ghosts, Dad?" she asked.

Pam's father winked at her. "I figure people blame the Warner ghost for their clumsiness in the woods," he answered. "If they fall off their horse, they say Warner did it. If they sprain their ankle slipping on wet leaves, it's Warner's fault."

Pam sighed with relief. Her smart, sensible father didn't believe in ghosts. He knew that they were just stories. He knew there was an explanation for everything.

The Pony Pals brought their sleeping bags up to the hayloft for their barn sleepover.

"We were in Mr. Warner's barn today," said Anna.

"No wonder it was spooky," added Lulu.

Pam stood at the hayloft door and stared out at the dark night sky.

Anna laid out her sleeping bag. "Mr. Warner's ghost was there," she said. "I felt him."

"It's so weird that we never saw that barn before," observed Lulu.

"It's haunted," said Anna.

Pam turned to her friends. "There's no evidence that there's a Warner ghost or that his barn is haunted," she declared.

"Lightning knows it's haunted," said Anna. She shook her finger at Pam. "And so do you."

Pam folded her arms. "You can't prove it," she said. "You don't have evidence."

Lulu stood between Anna and Pam and held up her hands. "Everybody calm down," she said. "This is a job for the Pony Pal Detectives. Let's make a list of clues."

"Okay," agreed Pam. "But we should only write down facts."

The girls sat around a hay-bale table and worked on the list. When they finished, Pam read their clues out loud.

IS THE WARNER BARN HAUNTED?
· Anna felt something in the barn, but nothing was there.
· The ponies were spooked.
· The barn door banged shut.
· The horseshoe over the doorway was hot.
· It was a clear day, but the sky looked cloudy from inside the barn.
· Pam heard a chain rattle and no one was there.
· Lightning tripped over nothing we could see.
· When we tried to go home, we ended up back at the barn.

"That list proves there is a ghost," said Anna.

"I think it proves that there *isn't* a ghost," said Pam. "There's a logical explanation for everything on that list. There's no ghost. There's no haunted barn."

"But you heard Warner's chain," said Anna. "Lightning was spooked and tripped. How do you explain that?"

Pam smiled. "It's simple," she said. "It was Tommy Rand and Mike Lacey."

Lulu and Anna exchanged a glance. They hadn't thought of Tommy and Mike.

Tommy Rand and Mike Lacey were older boys who were always playing tricks on the Pony Pals. Once they even stole their ponies.

"Maybe Mike and Tommy were following us," explained Pam. "Maybe they know about that barn. I bet they've heard the Warner ghost stories, too. They made the clanking noise."

"They could have banged the barn door closed," agreed Lulu.

"That's just the sort of thing Tommy and Mike would do," admitted Anna.

Pam closed her notebook. "So I'm right," she said. "The barn isn't haunted."

Anna reopened the notebook and pointed to the clue about the clouds. "Mike and Tommy can't make clouds appear and disappear," she said.

"Sometimes clouds move fast," said Pam.

Pam and Anna argued about the clues some more.

"What do you think, Lulu?" asked Pam.

Lulu stood up. "I haven't made up my mind," she said. She stretched and yawned. "And I'm too tired to think about it now."

A few minutes later, Anna and Lulu were in their sleeping bags. Pam turned off the light and slipped into hers.

"I want to hear more stories about the Warner ghost," said Anna.

"Me, too," agreed Lulu.

"Let's talk to Mr. Conway tomorrow," suggested Anna. "He's the expert on Morristown ghost stories."

Lulu and Pam agreed to interview Mr. Conway.

"I also want to go back to the barn," said Lulu. "Will you go back there, Pam?"

"Sure," answered Pam. "We can look for clues to prove that Mike and Tommy were there." She turned in her sleeping bag to face Anna. "What about you, Anna? Will you go back with us?"

"Yes," whispered Anna. "I want to find out if Mr. Warner is a nice ghost or a mean ghost."

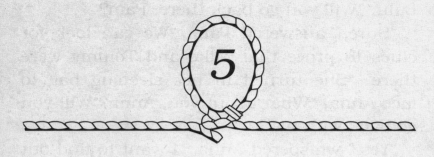

The Missing Pony

After breakfast the next morning, Anna and Lulu fed the ponies. Meanwhile, Pam went to the barn office to call Mr. Conway. His wife answered the phone.

"My husband is shoeing horses at Ms. Wiggins's place this morning," Mrs. Conway told Pam. Pam thanked her and hung up.

Pam ran out to the paddock to tell Lulu and Anna the good news. Ms. Wiggins was a good friend of the Pony Pals. She had great riding trails and the Pony Pals could ride there whenever they wanted.

"Perfect," said Anna. "Let's ride over there now and talk to Mr. Conway."

The girls saddled up their ponies.

Half an hour later they were at Ms. Wiggins's barn. Pam recognized the dark green pickup truck next to the barn. "Mr. Conway is here," she announced as she slid off Lightning.

"So is Mike Lacey," said Anna. "His bike is leaning against the barn."

Pam saw Mike's bike, too. Mike worked for Ms. Wiggins sometimes. He kept the trails cleared and helped in the barn and garden.

"Don't let Mike know why we're here," Pam whispered to Anna and Lulu.

They nodded in agreement.

The girls tied their ponies to the hitching post and went inside.

Mr. Conway was shoeing Ms. Wiggins's driving pony, Beauty.

The shiny black pony nodded at the Pony Pals. "Hi, Beauty," said Anna.

Lulu cleared her throat, but Mr. Conway didn't look at them.

The Pony Pals exchanged a glance. They were all remembering that Mr. Conway wasn't very friendly.

"I'm Pam Crandal, Mr. Conway," said Pam. "You take care of the ponies and horses at my mother's riding school."

"Yup," said Mr. Conway. He still didn't look up.

"Mrs. Conway told me you were here," explained Pam. "We came to talk to you."

Finally, Mr. Conway put down Beauty's back right hoof and looked up. "I remember you girls," he said. "All those questions about Morristown and ghosts."

"Can you tell us more about the Warner ghost?" asked Lulu.

"Why?" asked Mr. Conway. "He been up to his old tricks?"

"Sort of," said Anna.

The barn door opened and Mike Lacey walked in.

"Ms. Wiggins isn't here," he said when he saw the Pony Pals.

"They're here to see me," said Mr. Conway.

"They want to know about the Morristown ghosts. The ones I told you about."

Mike knows all about the Warner ghost, thought Pam, I was right. He and Tommy were out at the Warner barn scaring us.

"Please tell us everything you know about Mr. Warner," said Anna.

Mr. Conway picked up Beauty's front leg and took off the old shoe. "When people moved off the mountain," he began, "Warner stayed."

"All by himself?" asked Lulu.

"Some people like to be alone," answered Mr. Conway. "He had his animals."

Mike was cleaning out a stall, but he was listening, too.

"Mr. Warner must have come to town sometimes," said Lulu.

"Not after the fire," said Mr. Conway. He placed the new horseshoe against Beauty's hoof.

"What fire?" Anna and Mike asked in unison.

"Townspeople saw flames and smoke in the hills," Mr. Conway continued. "It was on the Warner property. The fire department took out the horse-drawn fire engine and headed on up there."

"What happened?" asked Anna.

"House burned to the ground," answered Mr. Conway. "Fire was licking at the barn. Firemen managed to put that one out. Warner saved his two cows and a horse." Mr. Conway patted Beauty's side. "But his carriage pony. They say his name was Storm. Well, Storm ran away."

"Did Mr. Warner move to town after the fire?" asked Lulu.

Mike looked up from sweeping out a stall. "He moved into the barn," he said. "Right, Mr. Conway?"

"Yup," agreed Mr. Conway. "Never left the mountain again. Years later a hiker found him dead. That's when the ghost stories started."

"Did he ever find Storm?" asked Anna.

"Nope," answered the farrier. He hammered in a horseshoe nail. "That's all I know about Warner."

"Did you ever see his ghost?" asked Anna. "Or feel him?"

"No one sees him," answered Mr. Conway. "That's the problem with some ghosts. But he tripped me up once. Sprained my ankle." He glared at the Pony Pals. "Now let me be. Warner's not the only one who likes to be alone."

"Thanks for talking to us, Mr. Conway," said Pam.

The Pony Pals headed out of the barn.

"Bye," Mike called out.

"Bye," Lulu and Anna called back.

Pam didn't say good-bye to Mike. He and Tommy had played tricks on them the day before. Now he was acting nice.

Mike has two different personalities, thought Pam. One is for when he's with Tommy. The other one is for the rest of the time.

"I told you it was Tommy and Mike," she

told Lulu and Anna when they were outside. "They know all the Warner ghost stories. They were trying to scare us."

"Maybe," agreed Lulu. "But I need more evidence."

"Let's go to the diner for lunch," suggested Anna. Her mother owned the diner, and it was a favorite hangout for the Pony Pals.

"But let's ride back to the barn afterward," added Lulu.

Ms. Wiggins was sitting at the diner counter. She smiled and waved at the Pony Pals. The girls went over to her. Pam told her that they had just been at her place.

"Did Mike tell you I was here?" she asked.

"He just said you weren't there," explained Lulu.

"Mike's been a great help to me," said Ms. Wiggins. "There's a lot of work to do in the fall."

"Did he work for you yesterday?" asked Pam.

"He did," said Ms. Wiggins. "Tommy Rand

was hanging around, which slowed him down. But Mike's still a good worker."

A woman came into the diner and waved to Ms. Wiggins. Ms. Wiggins said good-bye to the Pony Pals and went to a booth with her lunch date.

Mike and Tommy were at Ms. Wiggins's yesterday, thought Pam. They weren't at the Warner barn. A tingly feeling crept up her spine. There must be a logical explanation for what happened at the barn, Pam reminded herself. There has to be.

A Pile of Rocks

The Pony Pals went to their favorite booth in the back of the diner.

Pam and Lulu set the table while Anna ordered grilled cheese sandwiches, french fries, and apple juice for their lunch.

They had their Pony Pal meeting while they ate.

"Okay," said Pam. "We need a Pony Pal Plan. What are we going to do about that barn?"

Lulu passed the plate of french fries to Pam. "I want to go back to the barn and look for evidence," she said. "We need more proof that the barn is haunted."

"I want to prove that it *isn't* haunted," said Pam.

Anna was looking out the window at their ponies. "I already know it's haunted," she said. She turned to her friends. "And I just figured out something about Mr. Warner's ghost."

"What?" asked Pam and Lulu in unison.

"He's not a mean ghost," Anna said softly. "He's a sad ghost."

"Why do you think he's sad?" asked Lulu.

"His house burned down, and his driving pony disappeared," explained Anna. "That's why he's sad."

"But he tripped up Lightning," exclaimed Pam. "That's mean."

"I thought you don't believe in ghosts," said Anna.

"I don't," insisted Pam. "There is a logical explanation for everything that happened. You'll see."

* * *

After lunch, the girls rode back to Morristown. Lulu and Snow White led the way on the new trail. Anna and Acorn followed.

Pam urged Lightning forward. But Lightning didn't want to go on the new trail. "It's the trail you found yesterday," she reminded her pony.

Lightning finally followed the other ponies, but she was dancing sideways and snorting.

Anna suddenly halted Acorn. She turned in the saddle to face the other riders and put her fingers to her lips.

The three girls and their ponies stayed perfectly still and listened.

Pam heard a clinking noise.

Lightning backed up and whinnied.

The sound became louder. It was coming closer.

Snow White pawed the ground nervously.

Lulu dismounted. "Let's lead the ponies the rest of the way," she suggested.

The girls led their ponies quickly along the trail. The clinking, clanging sound followed them. Sometimes it was in front of them.

Sometimes it was behind them. But it was always coming from the woods.

The eerie sound stopped. Now the girls heard *OOOH-OOOH*.

"Is that an owl?" Pam asked Lulu.

"That's not a bird sound," answered Lulu.

"It's Mr. Warner's ghost," said Anna.

Pam heard another *OOOH-OOOH*. If I believed in ghosts, she thought, they would sound like that.

Lulu looked around nervously. "Should we go back?" she asked.

"I'm not afraid," said Anna.

"I'm not afraid, either," said Pam as she gripped the reins with her sweaty palms.

What if my dad heard these noises? she wondered. Would he believe in the Warner ghost? Would he be frightened?

"Let's keep going," said Lulu. "We're almost there."

The girls continued along the narrow trail. It ended at the row of maple trees.

"Look," gasped Lulu.

Pam looked between the trees. She saw the field. But the barn wasn't there.

"The barn is gone," said Lulu in amazement.

"This can't be the right field," said Pam. "We must have gotten lost again."

Anna walked over to Pam and pulled on her sleeve. "I just saw something red in the woods," she whispered. "The back of a jacket. And a bicycle. It's them."

Pam leaned toward Lulu. "Tommy and Mike are in the woods," she said in a low voice.

"Let's have an emergency meeting," whispered Lulu.

The girls moved their ponies in a circle and huddled in the center.

"Mike and Tommy are trying to scare us," whispered Pam. "I told you so."

"But the barn . . ." began Lulu.

"Forget the barn for now," said Pam. "We have to get back at Tommy and Mike."

"Let's scare them," suggested Anna.

A minute later, the Pony Pals had a plan. They mounted their ponies. Pam gave Anna the signal to begin.

"I'm so scared," shouted Anna. "The Warner ghost is following us. I'm never coming back here again."

Anna really sounds frightened, thought Pam. She's the best actress.

"Pam, you lead the way," said Lulu in a loud voice. "And go fast."

"Okay," agreed Pam. "Let's get out of here."

Pam rode her pony fast. When she was far ahead of the other riders, she stopped.

"Come on, Lightning," she said as she quickly dismounted. "We're hiding."

Pam led Lightning behind a big boulder. "Please be a good pony and don't make a sound," she said. Lightning lowered her head and nibbled on a small patch of grass.

Soon Lulu and Anna rode past them. Pam and Lightning stayed hidden.

A minute later, Pam saw Mike and Tommy on the other side of the trail. They were riding their mountain bikes through the woods. Tommy carried a bike chain and lock. It made a clinking, clanging noise when he shook it.

"OOH-OOH," called Mike.

Tommy rode out onto the trail and got off his bike. They were laughing hysterically.

"We scared them good," said Mike.

Okay, boys, thought Pam. It's my turn.

Pam made the *WHA-WHA* sounds of a crying baby.

Tommy stopped laughing. "Shh-shh," he told Mike. "What's that?"

"WHA-WHA," cried Pam again.

"It's the Crying Baby ghost," said Mike in a shaky voice, "the one Mr. Conway told us about."

"WHA-WHA," Pam cried louder.

"Let's get out of here," shouted Tommy.

Pam heard bike wheels peeling away in the dirt. She had to cover her mouth so she wouldn't laugh out loud.

Lightning whinnied softly as if to say, "That was fun."

Pam led Lightning back to the trail and mounted. She rode slowly so they wouldn't catch up with Mike and Tommy.

Anna and Lulu were waiting for Pam at the Ridley Farm ruin.

She told them that the trick worked. "Mike and Tommy were *so* scared," she giggled.

Lulu raised her hand and the Pony Pals hit high fives.

"I told you it was those guys scaring us yesterday," said Pam. She smiled at Anna. "So will you stop talking about ghosts?"

Anna didn't smile back. "Where's Mr. Warner's barn?" she asked.

"We didn't find it today because we went the wrong way," answered Pam. She looked at Lulu. "Right?"

"I can't figure out what went wrong," said Lulu. "I followed the map we made yesterday." She looked from Pam to Anna. "Let's try again."

Anna looked at her watch. "I have to go home," she said. "My reading tutor is coming this afternoon."

Lulu looked up at the sky. She could tell time by the position of the sun. "It's later than I thought," she said. "I have to go home, too. I promised my grandmother I'd rake the backyard."

"And I have to work the school ponies today," added Pam. "We better go."

As the Pony Pals rode, they continued to disagree about the ghost and barn. But they did agree on one thing. They'd have a Pony Pal Meeting in the Harley paddock the next morning. Each girl would have an idea about what to do next. Pam hoped her idea would prove that there wasn't any ghost in the barn.

Three Ideas

The next morning, Pam rode on Pony Pal Trail to meet Anna and Lulu. Pony Pal Trail was a mile-and-a-half trail through the woods. It went from the Crandals' big field to the Harleys' paddock.

Anna and Lulu were waiting for Pam in the paddock. They helped take off Lightning's tack and cool her down. Snow White watched. Acorn was busy rolling in the dirt.

"Let's have our meeting at the picnic table," suggested Anna.

The girls walked over to the table and sat

down. Anna's sketchbook was already there. Pam put her pad next to it.

"Okay," said Pam. "This is a meeting about the secret barn."

"We should call it the *hidden* barn," commented Lulu, "since we can't find it."

"It's a *haunted* barn," said Anna.

Pam glared at Anna. "You should have a more open mind," she said.

"So should you," snapped Anna.

"Okay, okay, you two," said Lulu. "We agree that you disagree. Now let's find out what's happening."

"What's your idea, Lulu?" asked Pam.

Lulu pulled a piece of paper from her jacket pocket. She handed it to Pam. Pam read it out loud.

Lulu's Idea
Go to the Historical Society to learn more about Mr. Warner.

"We already learned a lot about Mr. Warner from Mr. Conway," said Anna.

"The Historical Society might have some more facts about him," said Lulu.

"I think it's a good idea," said Pam. "I'm interested in sticking to the facts."

"All right," agreed Anna. "We'll go to the Historical Society."

"What's your idea, Anna?" asked Lulu.

Anna opened her sketchpad to a drawing and showed it to Lulu and Pam.

"I want to go back to the haunted barn," said Anna. "We should keep looking until we find it."

"I thought we went the right way yesterday," said Lulu.

"We made a mistake some place," said Pam. "Mike and Tommy distracted us with their tricks."

"They tricked us yesterday," said Anna. "But they didn't trick us on Saturday. Saturday Mike worked for Ms. Wiggins."

"That's what my idea is about," said Pam. She opened her notebook and handed it to Lulu. "Here. You read it."

Lulu read Pam's idea out loud.

PAM'S IDEA
  Mike only worked for Ms. Wiggins on Saturday morning. In the afternoon he and Tommy were in Morristown.

"How do you know, Pam?" asked Anna.

"Yesterday, Mike just worked in the morning," answered Pam. "In the afternoon he and Tommy followed us. I think that's what they did on Saturday, too."

"Did you ask Ms. Wiggins how long

Mike worked on Saturday?" asked Lulu.

"I tried," said Pam. "She wasn't home." She stood up. "I'll try again right now."

Pam ran across the yard and into Anna's house. She hoped Ms. Wiggins was home. I know I'm right about Mike and Tommy, she thought. She punched in Ms. Wiggins's phone number.

Ms. Wiggins answered after the third ring.

Pam told her that the Pony Pals had a question. "Mike Lacey worked for you on Saturday," said Pam. "But he only worked in the morning. Right?"

"Actually, he worked all day on Saturday," answered Ms. Wiggins. "Mike and Tommy didn't leave until dark. I made sure their bike lights worked. I didn't want them riding home at night without lights."

Pam thanked Ms. Wiggins. As she hung up the phone, Anna and Lulu walked into the kitchen.

"What did she say?" asked Lulu.

"Mike worked all day Saturday," reported Pam. "And Tommy was with him the whole time." She was glad that Anna didn't say *I told you so.*

"Let's ride to the Historical Society now," suggested Lulu.

"Then we'll go back to the barn," added Anna.

The girls walked across the Town Green to the Historical Society building. Pam wished she'd been right about Mike and Tommy. If they didn't spook them at Warner's barn, who or what did?

8

October 2

Ms. McGee, the director of the Historical Society, was on the front lawn. She wore a long dress and was raking leaves with a wooden rake. It was part of her job to do things in old-fashioned ways.

Ms. McGee smiled at the Pony Pals. "What can I do for you girls today?" she asked.

Lulu explained that they were looking for information on Mr. Warner.

"The one that's a ghost," explained Anna.

"But we're not interested in ghost stories,"

added Pam. "We've already heard enough of those. We want the facts."

"Thomas Warner was the last person to live in Morristown," said Ms. McGee. "His real-life story is a sad one."

"He was sad because his pony Storm ran away," said Anna. "And his house burned down. Right, Ms. McGee?"

"I see that you girls already know a lot about Mr. Warner," said Ms. McGee. "Come inside if you want to learn more."

The girls followed Ms. McGee into the building. She led them to the library.

"Lots of people have been interested in Thomas Warner," she explained. She pulled out the bottom drawer of a big file cabinet. "I've copied some old newspaper clippings and stories about him." She pulled a brown folder out of the file cabinet. "They're all in here," she said as she put the folder on the table.

"Thank you," said Pam and Anna in unison.

"Don't remove the file from the library," instructed Ms. McGee. "But you may make photocopies of anything you want to keep." She looked out at the sunny fall day. "I'm going back to my raking."

The Pony Pals sat side by side at the table.

Lulu read the tab on the side of the folder, "THOMAS WARNER, 1856 to 1910."

Pam opened the folder, and the girls looked at the top page.

"This is an article about ghost stories in Morristown," said Lulu. "It was written five years ago."

Pam pointed to the middle of the article. "There are two paragraphs on Mr. Warner," she said. "But they're about Warner the ghost, not Warner the person."

Anna picked up the article and silently read it.

Meanwhile, Pam and Lulu looked at the next page in the folder. "Here's another article about Morristown ghosts," she said.

"This one was written fifteen years ago," commented Lulu.

More ghost stories, thought Pam. She wondered if they would find any facts in the file.

Lulu turned to the next paper. "Here's a newspaper article from 1910," she said.

Pam looked the page over. The article wasn't about ghosts. It was an obituary announcing a death. The death of Mr. Thomas Warner.

Pam read the obituary out loud.

𝔚𝔦𝔤𝔤𝔦𝔫𝔰 𝔊𝔞𝔷𝔢𝔱𝔱𝔢

THOMAS WARNER 1856–1910

Mr. Thomas Warner, the last resident of Morristown, was found dead in the woods near his home on the morning of April 15. The body was discovered by Randolph Sears, a local hiker. Dr. Jackson reports that Mr. Warner suffered a heart attack while chopping wood. Thomas Warner lived alone. His wife, Janice Tilden Warner, and their four-year-old daughter, Tilly, died in 1896. After the tragic loss of his family, Mr. Warner rarely came to town.

Dr. Jackson was a childhood friend of Thomas Warner. "When Tom's wife and girl died, something died inside him as well," Dr. Jackson told the Gazette. "Lots of folks think he went strange when his house burned down. But it wasn't the fire that broke Tom's heart. It was the death of his wife and child."

The fire that destroyed Mr. Warner's house on October 2, 1896, also burned parts of his barn. Nevertheless, Warner lived in the damaged barn for the remainder of his life.

Prayer service will be held for Thomas Warner at the Episcopal Church this Saturday. Following the service, his remains will be buried beside those of his wife and daughter in the old Morristown cemetery. Thomas Warner was the son of James Warner and Ellen Smith Warner of Morristown. Both are deceased.

When Pam finished reading, the Pony Pals sat silently for a few seconds.

Anna was the first to speak. "His wife *and* his child died," she said. "That is so sad."

"I feel sorry for him," said Lulu. "People shouldn't joke about his ghost."

Anna turned to the next page in the vertical file. The title of the article was "A Hiker's Guide to a Real Ghost Town."

"Another article about ghost stories," complained Pam.

"Look," said Lulu. She pointed to an illustration in the article. "Here's a map for hikers. It's of Morristown."

The three girls studied the map.

Lulu put her finger on it. "There's Ridley Farm," she said. "And here's the trail we took. It was a wagon road and leads right to the Warner property."

Lulu picked up the article. "I'm going to photocopy the map," she said. "It might help us find the barn again."

While Lulu photocopied the map, Pam reread Mr. Warner's obituary to herself. She stopped when she came to the date of the fire. "What's today?" she asked Anna and Lulu.

"Monday," answered Anna.

"But what *date* is it?" said Pam.

"October fourth," Lulu answered.

Pam's heart thumped in her chest. "We went to the barn on October second," she said in a hoarse whisper.

The Pony Pals stared at one another in amazement. Lulu said aloud what they were all thinking. "We were there on the anniversary of the fire," she said.

"That's so spooky," said Anna.

Pam stood up. "We have to go back to the barn," she said. "We have to find it again."

Lulu and Anna agreed that it was time to go back to the barn.

As the girls walked across the Town Green, Pam felt sad. Poor Mr. Warner, she thought. He had a hard life.

Pam was glad that they were riding. She wanted to be close to her pony. Then she remembered the barn. What if we don't find it? she wondered. What would that mean?

Six Maple Trees

The Pony Pals went back to Anna's backyard. They put the hiker's map of Morristown on the picnic table. Lulu put the Pony Pal map they had drawn beside it.

"It's the same route to Warner's on both maps," observed Pam.

"We'll use them both," said Lulu, "and follow them exactly."

Pam and Lulu saddled up the ponies. Anna went inside to make them a picnic lunch.

Soon the Pony Pals were ready. They rode

their ponies up Anna's driveway and onto Main Street.

"Acorn! Acorn!" shouted a friendly girl.

Pam looked around. Mike Lacey and his sister, Rosalie, were walking across the Town Green. Rosalie was six years old, and Mike baby-sat for her a lot. Rosalie loved ponies, especially Acorn.

Rosalie ran over to the Pony Pals. Mike followed.

Pam didn't see Tommy Rand anywhere. Good, she thought. Maybe Mike will act like a human being.

Rosalie kissed Acorn on the cheek. "Can I have a ride?" she asked Anna.

"Not today," answered Anna. "We're going on a trail ride."

"Where are you going?" asked Rosalie.

"Morristown," answered Pam. She looked right at Mike when she said it.

He looked surprised. So did Rosalie. "Morristown!" she exclaimed. "There are ghosts in Morristown. Aren't you scared?"

"No," said Lulu. Now *she* was looking right at Mike.

"Maybe the ghosts are friendly," said Anna. "I'm not afraid of friendly ghosts."

Acorn nickered as if to say, "Me, neither."

"Mike heard a ghost yesterday," Rosalie said. "It was a *mean* ghost. It's called the Crying Baby ghost, only it's not a baby. It *pretends* to be a baby to trick people."

Pam and Lulu exchanged a glance. Pam coughed to hide a laugh. Lulu covered her mouth.

"We heard about that Crying Baby ghost," said Anna. "It's scary all right. I hope we don't run across it."

"That was just a story, Rosalie," said Mike. "You asked me to tell you a scary story."

"You said it *happened*, Mike," Rosalie insisted. "You *said*."

"Well, I wasn't scared," said Mike. He glared at the Pony Pals. "I wasn't."

You weren't scared, thought Pam. You were terrified!

Mike put his hand on his little sister's shoulder. "Come on," he said. "Let's go to the library. I'll race you."

Mike and Rosalie ran off across the Town Green.

The Pony Pals rode down Main Street. Pam noticed that Mike let Rosalie win the race. Sometimes he really can be nice, she thought.

When the three riders reached Mudge Road they stopped their ponies. They were still laughing about Mike and the Crying Baby ghost.

"You *really* scared him, Pam," said Lulu.

"He's not going back to Morristown for a long time," added Anna.

"But we are," said Lulu. "So let's go."

The girls rode along Mudge Road. It led to Riddle Road. Soon they were on the Morristown trail.

When they'd ridden for fifteen minutes, the girls stopped. Lulu took out the maps and studied them. "Okay," she said. "The trail to Warner's starts before the Ridley Farm." She put the maps in her pocket and rode onto the trail.

"Let's go, Acorn," said Anna. Acorn was happy to follow Snow White. But Lightning whinnied and tried to turn around. She wanted to go back.

"It's okay, Lightning," Pam said soothingly. "We've been here before. You found this trail."

Pam wondered what was upsetting Lightning. Did her pony know something she didn't know?

As they rode, Pam looked for landmarks. She finally saw the boulder she had hidden behind the day before. Lulu and Anna were still ahead of her.

Pam rode Lightning behind the boulder. Anna and Lulu didn't notice that she wasn't riding with them.

"WHA-WHA," Pam cried out from her hiding place. She sneaked a look at Anna and Lulu.

Anna pulled Acorn up short. She turned

in her saddle. Pam saw that she was star-tled.

Lulu rode up beside Anna. She could see Pam and that she was laughing.

"Okay, Pam," Lulu called. "Very funny!"

Pam rode out from behind the boulder. "WHA-WHA," she repeated.

"That's *real* scary," teased Anna.

"Save me from the Crying Baby ghost," giggled Lulu.

"That's where I hid yesterday," explained Pam. "I wanted to show you."

"So this *is* the trail we took yesterday," said Lulu.

"When we didn't find the barn," added Anna.

"Maybe we didn't ride far enough," said Pam. "Mike and Tommy distracted us."

"Maybe," agreed Lulu.

The girls rode on. The wide trail turned into a narrow trail. Lulu checked her maps again. "We should be there soon," she announced.

A few minutes later, the trail ended at a row of maple trees.

Pam and Anna rode up beside Lulu. There was a field on the other side of the trees.

"This looks like the same field we rode into yesterday," said Pam, "when we couldn't find the barn."

Lulu rode Snow White a few strides to the left and looked up at the treetops.

"This is where we were on Saturday, too," she said.

"How do you know?" asked Pam.

Lulu pointed up. "That tree," she answered. "On Saturday I noticed that one of the big branches was gone."

Pam looked up. A big branch was missing from one side of the tree.

Lulu pointed to a huge fallen branch at the foot of the tree. "I rode Snow White around that," she said.

"Lots of trees lose their branches," said Pam. "Maybe we should ride farther."

"The trail ends here," Lulu reminded her. She took out her binoculars and scanned the field.

Pam rode Lightning back onto the trail

and looked in all directions. Lulu was right. The trail ended at the maple trees.

"I see something," shouted Lulu.

Pam rode back to Lulu and Anna.

"There's a pile of rocks in the bushes at the end of the field," said Lulu. She handed the binoculars to Pam. "There's a stone wall, too. There was a building in this field."

Pam looked through the binoculars. Lulu was right. There was a ruin at the end of the field. It looked like the other ruins in Morristown.

"That's where the barn was," said Lulu. Her voice was shaking. "I'm sure of it."

"Let's check it out," said Anna.

"We'll look for clues," agreed Lulu. Her voice was steadier.

A shiver ran up and down Pam's spine. Her heart was pounding in her chest. She didn't want her friends to know she was spooked, too.

"Let's go," said Pam as she led the way toward the ruin.

The Dig

The Pony Pals rode to the other end of the field. They dismounted and tied their ponies to birch trees near the ruin.

Lulu walked along the sides of the foundation.

"This building was the size of the Warner's barn we were in," she said. She walked into the space. "And this was Warner's tack room."

"*If* this is his barn," added Pam.

Anna knelt down and parted tall grass with her hands. "Let's inspect every inch of this place," she said. "Maybe we'll find more clues."

Lulu picked up a flat rock. "We can dig with rocks," she said.

Pam found a sharp-edged rock and joined the search.

The girls worked side by side looking for clues.

Pam hoped it wasn't the Warner barn. She wanted to find a clue to prove that.

Her hand hit something. She held the grass back and looked more closely. A piece of wood was sticking up out of the ground.

"I found something," she announced.

Anna and Lulu ran over. Pam pulled at the wood, but it didn't budge.

"It must be bigger underneath than it is on top," commented Lulu.

"Like an iceberg," added Anna.

"Let's dig it out," suggested Pam.

Pam and Lulu dug carefully around the piece of wood. When the earth was loose, they pulled it out.

Pam brushed dirt off the surface of the wood.

Lulu touched one end. "This wood is charred," she said. "It was in a fire."

Anna looked carefully at the other end of the board. "Something is written on it," she said in a hushed voice.

"R-N-E-R," read Lulu.

"That's the end of Warner," said Anna. "This was part of Mr. Warner's tack trunk. The lettering is the same."

"A lot of names end in R-N-E-R," said Pam.

Lulu sat back on her heels and looked around. "This *is* the Warner barn," she said. "We were here on Saturday. Only it wasn't a ruin."

Anna sat on the rock wall. "It was a ghost barn," she said.

Pam looked at the piece of wood. Was it from Mr. Warner's trunk?

"Maybe we dreamed we were here," said Pam. "Maybe we all had the same dream."

"If you believe that," said Lulu, "you might as well believe in ghosts."

"Face it, Pam," said Anna. "Thomas Warner is a ghost and so is his barn. We were in a *ghost* barn."

"I just thought of something else," exclaimed Lulu. "Maybe that horseshoe was too hot to touch because of the fire."

Lightning whinnied. Pam stood up to see why. Her pony's ears were pointed forward. "She heard something," Pam told Anna and Lulu.

Snow White's ears were forward, too. All three ponies were facing the row of maple trees.

"What did you hear?" Pam called to Lightning.

"Shush," said Anna. "Listen."

Everyone stayed perfectly still and listened.

A few seconds later they heard a clinking, clanging sound.

"That's what I heard on Saturday," whispered Pam.

"It sounds like harness bells," said Lulu.

The sound was coming closer. Pam listened.

"You're right," she told Lulu. "It's the bells on a harness. Someone is driving a pony."

"Mr. Warner is driving Storm!" exclaimed Anna. "His pony is a ghost, too!"

Lightning whinnied. A distant whinny answered her.

"They're riding toward us," said Anna excitedly. "They're riding to the barn." Her eyes were wide with excitement and fear.

Lulu covered her eyes. "I'm too scared to look," she said.

Pam ran out of the ruin. I will not be afraid, she told herself. I *do not* believe in ghosts.

Her heart pounding, Pam made herself look toward the maple trees. She saw a carriage and rider between the tree trunks. Was it a ghostly apparition?

"I am not afraid," Pam repeated to herself. Anna and Lulu came up beside her.

Pam saw the pony and driver more clearly

now. She jumped up and down excitedly and waved. Ms. Wiggins was driving Beauty across the field toward them.

"There's your ghost and his ghost pony!" exclaimed Pam.

Lightning whinnied a cheerful hello to Beauty. Beauty answered.

Pam laughed. "I told you there was no such thing as ghosts," she told Anna and Lulu.

"What about the barn?" asked Lulu.

"I don't know," said Pam. "We'll figure it out later." She didn't want to think about the barn. *That* was really scary.

Ms. Wiggins pulled up beside them. "The Pony Pals are here," she said. "What a nice surprise."

Pam remembered the clinking harness bells she heard on Saturday. "Were you driving Beauty around here on Saturday?" she asked Ms. Wiggins.

"I haven't driven here in more than a year," answered Ms. Wiggins. She looked around. "I love Morristown in the fall, especially this field."

Ms. Wiggins climbed out of the carriage to stretch her legs. Pam stroked Beauty's shiny black coat.

Anna and Lulu told Ms. Wiggins about the barn they saw on Saturday.

"Now there's just a ruin here," concluded Lulu.

"That's all I've ever seen here," said Ms. Wiggins.

"I think we found a different barn on Saturday," said Pam. "We just can't find it again."

"It was a real barn," added Anna. "It wasn't a ruin."

"But there aren't any barns like that around here," said Ms. Wiggins. "There are only ruins."

"It was a haunted barn," Anna said. "Mr. Warner is a powerful ghost. He has a ghost pony and cart that he drives. And a ghost barn."

"Do you believe in ghosts?" Pam asked Ms. Wiggins.

"Not generally," she answered.

"Me, neither," said Pam.

"But whenever I ride in these woods, Pam," Ms. Wiggins continued, "I feel the spirits of the people of Morristown. It's like they are still here. All those good people and the animals they loved."

Lulu and Anna smiled and nodded.

Ms. Wiggins climbed back in her carriage. "Do you girls want to ride back with me?" she asked.

Lulu looked back at the ruin. "I'm ready to go," she said.

"Me, too," said Pam.

"Me, three," said Anna.

Ms. Wiggins led the way onto the trail. Pam turned in the saddle and took a last look at the field. She knew it was the field they had visited on Saturday. She wondered if she would ever understand what happened to the barn or what brushed by her in the paddock that rainy night.

She leaned over and hugged Lightning. "I'm not sure I believe in ghosts," she whispered to her pony. "But if I ever meet one, I hope it's a nice ghost."

Dear Reader,

I am having fun researching and writing the Pony Pal books. I've met great kids and wonderful ponies at homes, farms, and riding schools. Some of my ideas for Pony Pal adventures have even come from these visits!

I remember the day I made up the main characters for the series. I was walking on a country road in New England. First, I decided that the three girls would be smart, independent, and kind. Then I gave them their names—Pam, Anna, and Lulu. (Look at the initial of each girl's name. See what it spells when you put them together!) Later, I created the three ponies. When I reached home, I turned on my computer and started to write. And I haven't stopped since!

My friends say that I am a little bit like all of the Pony Pals. I am very organized, like Pam. I love nature, like Lulu. But I think that I am most like Anna. I am dyslexic and a good artist, just like her.

Readers often wonder about my life. I live in an apartment in New York City near Central Park and the Museum of Natural History. I enjoy swimming, hiking, painting, and reading. I also love to make up stories. I have been writing novels for children and young adults for more than twenty years! Several of my books have won the Children's Choice Award.

Many Pony Pal readers send me letters, drawings, and photos. I tape them to the wall in my office. They inspire me to write more Pony Pal stories. Thank you very much!

I don't ride anymore and I've never had a pony. But you don't have to ride to love ponies! And you certainly don't need a pony to be a Pony Pal.

Happy Reading,

Jeanne Betancourt